Rosie's Hat

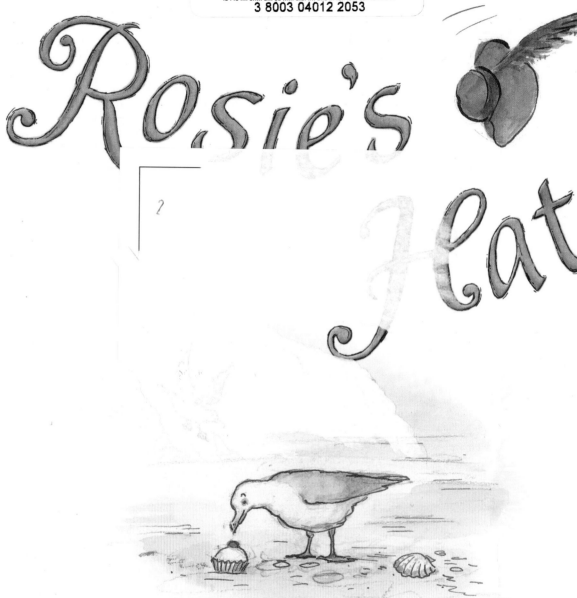

Written by Julia Donaldson

Illustrated by Anna Currey

Macmillan Children's Books

The wind blows high, the wind blows low.
PUFF, PUFF! BLOW, BLOW!

Rosie's hat blows off a cliff.
BOO-HOO! SNIFF, SNIFF!

A feather flutters on the breeze.
TICKLE, TICKLE! SNEEZE, SNEEZE!

The dog wakes up and sees the hat.
WOOF, WOOF! WHAT'S THAT?

Dog grabs hat and makes a dash.
PAD, PAD! SPLASH, SPLASH!

A fisherman has caught the hat.
BOTHER, BOTHER! DRAT, DRAT!

A screech owl flies above the beach.
FLAP, FLAP! SCREECH, SCREECH!

A mouse escapes an open beak.
PATTER, PATTER! SQUEAK, SQUEAK!

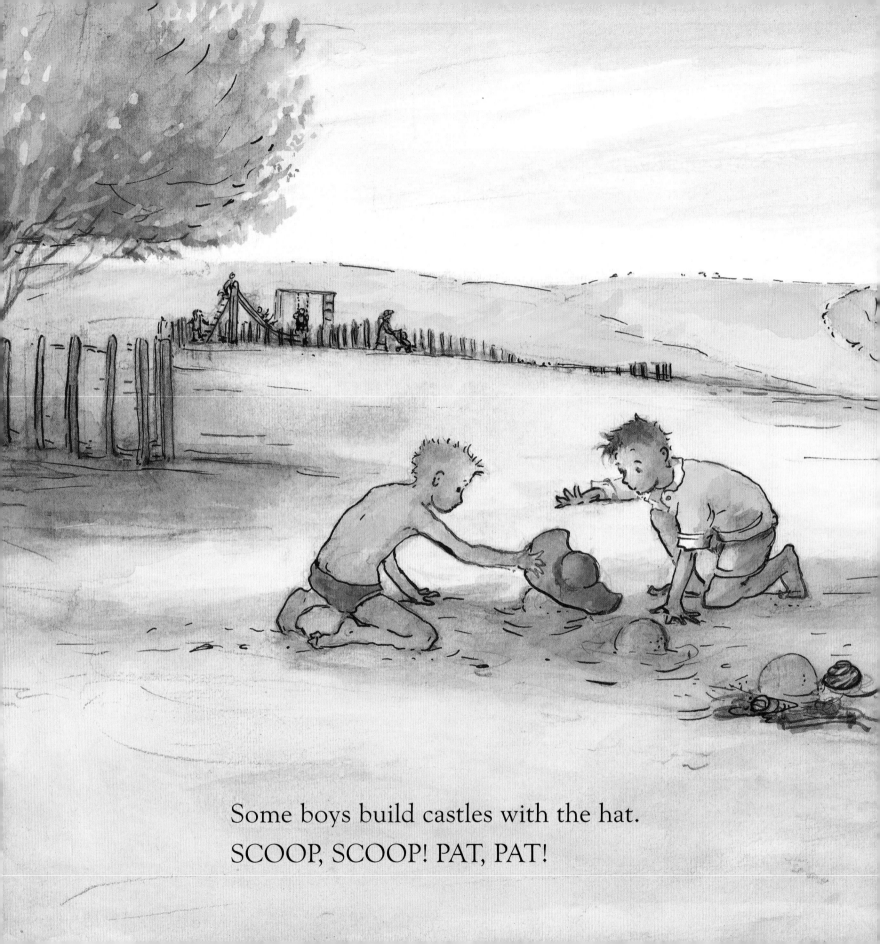

Some boys build castles with the hat.
SCOOP, SCOOP! PAT, PAT!

The hat is tossed into a tree.
ONE, TWO, THREE, WHEE!

Years go by, and little Rose

GROWS …

GROWS …

GROWS . . .

and GROWS.

Baby birds like worms to eat.
TWITTER, TWITTER! TWEET, TWEET!

The babies grow as weeks go by.
FLUTTER, FLUTTER! FLY, FLY!

Watch out, bird – here comes a cat.
WRIGGLE, POUNCE! HOWZAT?

Dog meets cat – whatever now?
WOOF, WOOF! MIAOW, MIAOW!

Stuck in a tree? You poor old thing!
BLEEP, BLEEP . . .

... BRRRING, BRRRING!

The rescue lady comes . . . it's Rose!
UP, UP! HERE GOES!

She's at the top! She's got the cat!
WELL, WELL! FANCY THAT …

FANCY THAT! IT'S ROSIE'S HAT!

Here's a feather – stick it in!
SAY CHEESE! GRIN, GRIN!

Here's a funny photograph.

GIGGLE, GIGGLE! LAUGH, LAUGH!

For Mary ~ J.D.
For Gill and Jessie, with love ~ A.C.

First published 2005 by Macmillan Children's Books
This edition published 2006 by Macmillan Children's Books
a division of Macmillan Publishers Ltd
20 New Wharf Road, London N1 9RR
Basingstoke and Oxford
Associated companies throughout the world
www.panmacmillan.com

ISBN: 978-1-4050-0007-9

Text copyright © Julia Donaldson 2005
Illustrations copyright © Anna Currey 2005
Moral rights asserted.

7 9 8 6

A CIP catalogue record for this book is available from the British Library

Printed in Belgium by Proost